Raymond
meets the Queen

For Isobel and Scarlett,
Enjoy Raymond's journey.
Best Wishes,
Janet Gibbs
24/4/17

Written and illustrated
by Janet Gibbs

First published in 2017 by Janet Gibbs

Copyright © 2017 Janet Gibbs

All rights reserved. No part of this publication may be reproduced, stored in a retrieval system or transmitted in any form or by any means, electronic, mechanical, photocopying and recording or otherwise, without permission in writing by the publisher.

Janet Gibbs has asserted her moral right to be identified as the author and illustrator of this work.

A CIP catalogue record for this book is available from the British Library.

ISBN: 978-0-9957898-0-7

For Joyce and Peter with love

 # Contents

Chapter One
A family gathers

Chapter Two
Raymond packs his case

Chapter Three
Raymond on the train

Chapter Four
Raymond at the palace gates

Chapter Five
Raymond sneaks in!

Chapter Six
Raymond meets his match!

Chapter Seven
Raymond meets the Queen!

Chapter Eight
Raymond gets his wish!

Chapter One

A family gathers

Raymond sat with his back against the old apple tree. The day was hot and he was glad of the shade. School had just finished and the summer holidays stretched invitingly ahead. Now, he could sleep and dream. When he wasn't dreaming, Raymond often had his nose in a book. Adventure stories were best. Tales of giants, dragons and pirates thrilled him to the core. He closed his eyes and was just beginning to imagine himself in a fierce battle, pitting his wits against a deadly foe, when a sudden shout forced him awake.

He looked up to see his sister Clarissa charging up the path in that silly tutu she liked to wear! 'Something's up!' she panted. 'Father's called a meeting — you're to come at once!' She rolled her eyes dramatically.

'Something's up!'

Raymond got up. He felt sure she'd got it wrong. But as they approached the sitting room door, he began to feel uncomfortable. Not even the smell of mother's freshly-baked scones could comfort him. He turned the handle and went in.

Father stood in front of the mantelpiece, his hands behind his back, always a bad sign. On his right, his darling mother with baby George on her lap, on his left, his grandparents, Papa and Maisie Mackenzie. They all sat stiffly and looked ahead.

Alone on the Persian rug, Raymond stood and waited.

'A family gathers'

'It's not good news' father said. 'Sales have plummeted. Unless we take action, we'll be out on the streets!'

The Mackenzie Cheese Company originally set up by Papa Mac made robust, flavoursome cheeses.

The factory was situated in Kensal Rise, London, and Raymond sometimes helped out, learning from his grandfather all about the different cheeses and how they were made.

He loved watching Papa Mac in action and admired the way he could persuade tricky clients to spend their money.

His grandmother Maisie Mackenzie had created the original recipes at her kitchen table in Scotland many years ago.

The decision to move south to London in the hope of attracting wealthy customers had been successful. Now, sadly, things had changed. This explained father's unhappy look.

'So' and here he paused to look at Papa Mackenzie. 'We've come up with a plan.'

Raymond shifted uncomfortably. He couldn't see where this was going. 'Why involve me?' he pondered. The answer came soon enough.

'You're to go to Buckingham Palace, see the Queen and ask her to grant us a Royal Warrant…'

'What on earth is that?' asked Raymond.

'Well,' said his father. 'If the Queen likes our cheeses, she can give us special permission to sell them to her!'

'Oh!' said Raymond. 'Does that mean more people will buy from us?'

'Precisely, Raymond' he replied.

'Now, listen carefully. We've selected our finest cheeses for Her Majesty to taste'…

'But father, how on earth am I to get past the guards?'

'It's simple. Go around to the back door, you're thin enough, you'll find a way in!'

From his pocket, father pulled out a piece of paper.

'We've drawn a map for you so you don't get lost. Your Uncle Archie works in the kitchens. Once inside he'll direct you to the royal apartments … the rest is up to you!'

Raymond took the sheet dumbly. He dared not look at his mother.

'There's no time to lose. You're to set off to-morrow. Your mother will help you pack!'

And with that, he turned on his heel and left the room.

Chapter Two

Raymond packs his case

Back in his room, Raymond lay on his bed. 'Why me?' he moaned. His head hurt and he felt sick. A knock at the door made him sit up. Raymond sighed.

'Oh mother' he cried, 'I can't do what father wants. I'm not brave enough!'

'Yes, you are!' she replied, hugging him. 'Papa Mac has taught you well and you've a fine gift for words Raymond. I just know you'll charm the Queen into helping us!'

From the top of his wardrobe, she took down a solid leather suitcase, snapped open the locks and looked inside.

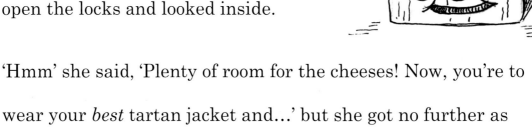

'Hmm' she said, 'Plenty of room for the cheeses! Now, you're to wear your *best* tartan jacket and…' but she got no further as Clarissa burst into the room.

'It's not fair!' she stormed, 'Why can't I go?'

Mother clapped her hands.

'That's enough, Clarissa! We've not much time and I must help Raymond pack. Please, please, go to your room!'

As Clarissa flounced out, Papa Mac glided in, his arms full of cheeses. Among them were three of his favourites:-

'Balmoral Blue', 'Heather Breeze' and 'Tam o' Shanter.'

Raymond looked up at his grandfather.

'Papa Mac, have *you* ever been afraid?'

Raymond waited.

'Oh, yes, especially when I had to face a cat for the first time. The thing to remember, my boy, is this: most cats are evil and want to see you on their dinner plate. Others are just plain stupid and slow and soon give up the chase.'

'Bad breath'

'My first battle was with a cat called Bruce. He was a foul creature, all big teeth and bad breath; his mistress, a bossy harridan*, liked to kick him around the room.' He went on.

'He'd lost an eye in combat as a youngster and that made him slower than most! I ran circles round him till he got so dizzy, he fell over. Then I bit his tail for all it was worth and shot off into the bushes!'

He beamed broadly.

'That did the trick, he never bothered me again!'

'Oh, Papa Mac' breathed Raymond, 'I believe I can triumph after all!' Then they all got up and went in for their tea.

*A woman who speaks sharply

Chapter Three

Raymond on the train

Saying 'Good-bye' to his family was the hardest part. With a heavy heart Raymond trudged miserably up the road to the station. The thump of feet on pavements made him shudder and once or twice, he came near to being trampled on by the press of people on their way to work. The roar of traffic, honking of horns and the screech of brakes rang in his head and almost made him turn back. Still he pressed on.

Slipping neatly under the ticket barrier at the station, he raced towards the escalator, watching and wondering if he would ever manage to get on this noisy, clanking beast. Taking a deep breath, he stepped on, trying not to fall over as it rattled and shook its way downwards.

At the bottom, one of his claws got stuck in its grooves, but he managed to yank it free and get off just in time! Now he hurtled forward and lost his balance, dropping his case. 'Oh, no!' he groaned, picking it up hastily and pressing it to his chest.

On the platform at last Raymond waited. He was hot and exhausted. As the train's roar echoed along the shadowy tunnel and rumbled into view, lights flashing, Raymond felt as if a huge monster was coming to get him.

Suddenly, from nowhere, a voice boomed:-

'Mind the gap between the train and the platform!'

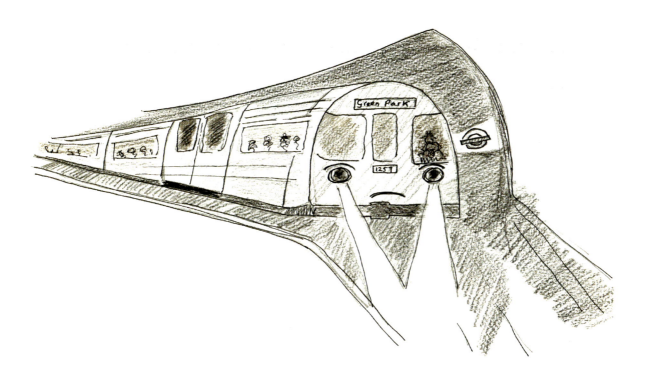

Sure enough, he looked across and saw a vast chasm open up between himself and the train and caught sight of thick metal tracks which gleamed sleekly below him. The doors slid open — there was nothing for it but to leap across, rolling over and hitting his head against a large, black boot!

Now he sat up, his nose twitching at the carriage's musty smell and peered through the legs in front of him. Slowly he crept forward and poked out his nose.

'A mouse, a mouse!' shrieked a lady scrambling onto her seat in terror.

All heads turned and several pairs of eyes stared in amazement.

'Oh, oh' she went on, 'I'm going to faint!'

A deep voice cut across her screams.

'Stop yer hollerin', and sit dahn, 'e won't bite!'

A rough-looking fellow in a flat hat bent down and grinned at Raymond. He looked at his tartan jacket and tiny suitcase and announced to the carriage:-

'I've seen a few in mi time, but this one's a class act. What's yer name, sonny?'

Raymond stood up.

'My name's Raymond Mackenzie, sir!'

'Pleased to meet yer, I'm Bert'. They shook hands.

'Where's you off to, then?'

'Well, actually,' he paused dramatically, 'I'm going to see the Queen!'

Voices babbled, someone laughed!

'Of course' Raymond went on 'I'd be awfully grateful if you could show me the way?'

'I go past Buck'nam Palace every day, it'll be a pleasure!'

Bert put the little case in his pocket and sat Raymond on his shoulder. With a jaunty air, they slipped through the doors like old friends, skipped up the stairs and emerged onto the streets of London.

Chapter Four

Raymond at the palace gates

People of all shapes and sizes hurried past them, looking grumpy and tired. Hanging onto Bert's collar, Raymond relished the fresh air and sun on his face. For the first time since he'd left home that morning, he allowed some of the terror and drama of his journey to slip away from him. Looking about him he cried out 'My word, London's a big place!'

'Yeah,' said Bert, 'specially when you're a mouse! Fancy a bacon butty? I always 'ave one before work!'

At the refreshment kiosk, Bert placed his order.

'Hello Len, a cuppa tea and a bacon butty for me and me mate 'ere!' — pointing to Raymond.

Len blinked in surprise.

'What yer doin' wiv the likes of 'im?' he said.

'He ain't no ordinary mouse, 'e's off to see the Queen.'

Len laughed and looked doubtful.

Bert fed Raymond scraps of his bacon roll. They tasted absolutely delicious. In all the fright of getting on the train, he'd completely forgotten his hunger. As they walked Raymond was full of questions.

'What's in your bucket, Bert?'

'Why,' said Bert 'Them's me cloths. I'm a winder cleaner, see!'

'But how on earth do you reach the windows at the very top?'

'Well' he replied 'I sit in a special box that goes up and down on ropes. It's quite safe!' He paused then went on.

'Some 'fings I seen would make yer 'air curl. Once, I saw two monkeys shut up in a kitchen. They was both sat up at the table, cool as you like, eating their cornflakes. Wiv' spoons an' all, munching away as if it was quite normal. I nearly died!' He laughed. 'Golly' said Raymond, 'how very peculiar!'

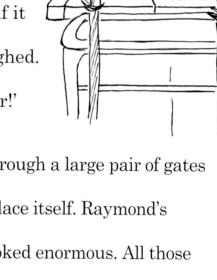

They passed graceful plane trees, went through a large pair of gates and soon were in front of Buckingham Palace itself. Raymond's heart began to beat hard. The building looked enormous. All those windows, row upon row of them and not a friendly face to be seen.

He wondered how many bedrooms there were, bathrooms too, not to mention staircases. On the roof, the Royal flag flapped cheerfully. 'You're in luck, mate' said Bert. 'She's at home!'

Cars whooshed past, the noise drummed in his ears.

Tourists gawped and pointed excitedly at the guards resplendent in their bearskin hats and brilliant red jackets. They stood eerily still, looking ahead as if their eyes were fixed on a distant point far above the bustling crowds.

'Bert, I have to go now!'

'Well, my friend, you've yer job to do and so 'ave I. If ever you're in trouble, send a message to me at *'The Dog and Bone'* on Piccadilly. I'll come straight away!'

He lowered Raymond gently down and handed him his case.

'Good luck, mate' and away he sauntered, swinging his pail.

Raymond stood for a moment, ignoring the hubbub around him.

Quietly, he slipped underneath the gilt-tipped railings and flattened himself against a wall.

He was inside the gates at last! No-one had seen him go and no-one cared. Trembling, he sat down on his case and planned his next move…

Chapter Five

Raymond sneaks in!

Raymond looked ahead. The palace loomed above him, larger than ever. In front of him, the guards on the forecourt paced slowly to and fro. Their sentry boxes stood one each side of a gigantic arch, through which he could see more buildings. Looking at father's map, he reckoned if he got through the archway, he could somehow find his way down to the kitchens and Uncle Archie.

Behind him, he heard the chatter of the crowd. A small boy, perched on his father's shoulder, cried out 'But daddy, I want to see the Queen *now*!'

And then as if by magic, the French windows on the royal balcony opened and figures began to appear. The sun glinted on colourful hats and satin dresses.

Stiff-suited men stood to attention, as the Queen herself, took centre stage, gorgeously arrayed in sparkling turquoise while with white-gloved hands she waved to her people.

It was now or never. With all eyes on the Queen, Raymond picked up his case and ran. He neared the sentry boxes and could see his way ahead but one of the sharp-eyed guards spotted his scurrying figure and ran after him shouting, 'Stop thief!'

Around the corner and up some stairs Raymond panted, hearing the thump of heavy boots behind him, till something sharp poked him in the back and he found himself being hauled high into the air.

'Gotcha, yer little guttersnipe!' crowed the guard.

And there, Raymond hung by his jacket, at the end of a bayonet, a sorry sight indeed. The game was up!

'Oh sir' he gasped 'Please, *please* let me go!'

'Now, why would I do that sonny?'

'Oh sir, please sir, my uncle is Archibald Mackenzie and…' he got no further.

The guard burst out laughing. He looked closely at Raymond with his neat tartan jacket and little brown suitcase. Something inside him softened.

'Well, well, I'd never live it down if I killed Archie's nephew' and so saying, he snatched open a side door and shouted through. A footman in soft slippers came running.

The guard barked an order.

'Take him down to the kitchens. He's one of Archie's own!'

He lowered Raymond to the ground who stammered a heartfelt

'T-t-hank-you!'

'Thomas, the Footman'

The guard turned on his heel with an 'I'd best git back to mi post' as Raymond followed the footman inside.

His feet slipped on marble floors as they sank lower and lower, down dark staircases, into the bowels of the palace itself.

Standing before a sturdy oak door, the footman paused. At his knock, a voice rumbled 'Enter!'

****

'Here's your nephew come to see you, Archie' said the footman as Raymond stepped forward. 'Thank-you Thomas!' he replied.

Raymond looked about him. Nothing had prepared him for this!

On a platform, beneath a silken canopy, his uncle sat on a velvet chair, puffing happily on a pipe. On his head he sported a little purple hat from which dangled a large black tassle. In his other hand, he fingered a gold pocket watch which hung from his waistcoat.

'*Archie's throne room*'

Brightly coloured rugs lined the walls. A lamp burned low. On a small table stood a majestic hookah*, while on a rack nearby, pipes of varying sizes waited to be smoked. The air smelt sweet and mellow.

'Well, well, let's have a look at you. Turn around!'

Raymond did as he was told.

'My, my, whatever happened to your tail?'

'During a fight with my sister, she shut it in the sitting room door. It's never been the same since' said Raymond sadly.

'Has your father ever spoken of me? No?' He took a few puffs.
'I ran away to sea at fifteen, by way of a cargo boat bound for the East. I got to like travelling and as you can see, I've picked up a few things along the way.'

*A hookah – is a type of Turkish pipe

'Now I'm older, I want an easy life. On my travels, I got to taste all different kinds of food and often helped the chef on board ship prepare meals. That's how I got the job of 'Royal Food Taster' to Her Majesty, Queen Elizabeth II' he said proudly.

Raymond looked puzzled.

'I make sure all her food tastes good and wholesome. If I become ill, it's no big deal, but Her Majesty remains safe and healthy.'

Suddenly, out of nowhere, a telephone shrilled. Archie picked up its sleek receiver.

'Primrose 2041.'

A pause.

'Is that you Mr. Mackenzie?' came a soft voice.

'Why, hello Queen' he replied. Silence. 'Ah, yes, as you wish Your Majesty, it shall be done!'

'Come, Raymond, I've to taste her supper tray before it gets sent up' and with a hop and a skip, he darted out into the hot, steamy kitchens nearby.

With great ceremony, Archie tasted each portion of food. Chewing thoughtfully, he nodded his approval to the chef, who ticked off a checklist as proof that all was as it should be for

Her Majesty. Wiping his mouth on a snowy napkin, Archie waved the tray away.

'It's your turn now. Tell me what your father has sent you to do…'

'This tastes grand!'

'Well, Uncle Archie, it's like this. Our business *The Mackenzie Cheese Company* isn't doing too well. I need to ask the Queen for a Royal Warrant. That would get us new customers and make father smile again. My job is to make sure Her Majesty tastes our best cheeses. So do you think you can show me where to find her?'

At last, Raymond was led to a grand staircase and Archie pointed ahead.

'Up there, turn sharp left, go down a long corridor and you'll find 'The Blue Sitting Room' at the end. In half an hour, Bunce the head butler will take up her tray. You can slip in then.'

'Oh, uncle, how can I *ever* thank you?' breathed Raymond. This was all going swimmingly.

'A word of warning, though' and here he paused dramatically. 'Watch out for Dennis!'

'Oh' said Raymond casually, 'Who's Dennis?'

'You'll soon find out!' and patting Raymond on the head, he skipped away back to his shadowy den.

Chapter Six

Raymond meets his match!

At the top of the stairs, Raymond paused. He found himself in a long gallery which seemed to stretch for miles.

Looking up, row on row of glass baubles winked at him, making him blink. His mouth opened in a soft 'Oh!' as he stared at a magnificent, sparkling, chandelier which hung rather precariously, from a single, twisted chain above him.

'I hope it doesn't fall down' he murmured as he carried on, stopping beneath a heavily-framed picture which took up one wall.

A stern gentleman in tight trousers and a flowing coat stared down at him, fat eyes bulging. In one hand he fingered a nasty-looking whip. Just looking at him made Raymond nervous.

He passed more paintings, cabinets with china plates on top of them and elaborate clocks which ticked mournfully in their gold frames. Outside the door marked 'The Blue Sitting Room' Raymond glanced around. He pushed his little case with its precious cargo underneath a chest of drawers, lay down and waited.

Suddenly, his nose twitched in alarm and his ears, always sharp, heard a scratching sound on the carpet ahead of him.

More worrying though was that all-too-familiar tingling in his tail which warned of a predator nearby. He remembered Uncle Archie's last words 'Watch out for Dennis!' — he should have known — this was the palace cat — who else?

****

Dennis was a handsome cat, no question. Striped from top to toe with broad orange markings, his long, shapely limbs were sinuous and strong. Visitors gasped in admiration as he loped across palace lawns in search of prey. Once he had an animal in his grasp, there was no escape. His electric green eyes, fringed with sweeping lashes, had a trick of looking through you and out the other side.

He had been principal rat catcher at Prince Charles's school. Unfortunately for Dennis, some of the older boys used him as target practice, cruelly pelting him with flinty stones from their

catapults. Taking pity, Prince Charles smuggled him home in his tuck box one half-term. Surprisingly, his mother took a shine to him and he was therefore installed in comfy quarters not far from the kitchens!

Then one day, he came up against Primo, the Queen's head corgi, out for his daily constitutional. They met head on in the covered walk.

War was instantly declared. Although Primo's legs were short he moved with startling speeds and could even jump quite high when pushed!

Having chased Primo up against a high wall in the kitchen gardens, Dennis felt he was getting the upper hand at last.

There they crouched, teeth bared, hissing and snarling, waiting for the other one to give way and admit defeat…

Suddenly Primo lunged forward and sank his teeth into Dennis's left ear; no matter that Dennis scratched and clawed at him, drawing blood, Primo hung on. No amount of scolding by the Queen could shift him until the head gardener saved the day by pouring ice-cold water over the combatants and peace was restored at last.

Thereafter Dennis became bad-tempered and unpredictable. His ear healed but remained a messy lump, greatly hurting his pride. He took to displaying in his den, all the trophy tails of his victims. Rats, mice, voles and weasels, he knew them all!

At state banquets, Dennis loved to cause the maximum discomfort to royal guests. Slipping underneath damask tablecloths, he would view all ankles on display and make a selection. A sharp nip just enough to make holes in a silk stocking or an ivory sock was enough. The resulting shrieks and cries of rage restored his good humour.

At night, he prowled the palace battlements with a proprietary air. In the moonlight, he would look down at imaginary crowds, shake his paws and declare 'I'm the real power behind the throne!'

Now, as he approached the long corridor, the smell of mouse came to him. His eyes sparkled meanly and his mouth watered. 'And now for some *FUN!*' he declared.

****

From his look-out post, Raymond fairly shook at the sight of Dennis. He was magnificent!

'I say, old bean, don't even try to escape! 'Dennis called, 'I'm coming to get you!'

Raymond's heart began to thump. He would have to be sharp to outwit this beast. Making the first move, he began to zig-zag from one side of the gallery to the other, up and down, back and forth, over and over again at lightning speed. He made sure to pause for a couple of minutes each time, teasing Dennis, then off he'd go again. There was a nasty moment when he felt a claw-like stab at his tail, but thankfully, he managed to wriggle free.

He laid low under a glass cabinet to catch his breath, and thought for a moment that he had company, but it was nothing more than a toy mouse, abandoned by Prince George on one of his visits to his great-grandmamma. It sat on four wheels, its face fixed in a stiff grin.

Gingerly, Raymond picked it up and turned the small knob. The wheels whirred noisily so that he dropped it in alarm; whereupon it shot out onto the carpet and whizzed crazily up the corridor, with Dennis in hot pursuit!

Raymond seized this chance to change tack. He scampered across the hall and shinned smartly up a thick bell-pull. There he hung for all the world like a seasoned trapeze artist, swinging expertly to and fro. From his superior position, he felt it was safe to torment Dennis.

'Tee-hee, can't catch me' he teased, boldly.

Furious, Dennis could only watch and wait.

'I say, old fruit' he mimicked, 'what have you done to your ear?'

This was a step too far. Dennis leapt into the air, slashing angrily at the swinging cord.

'Tee-hee, can't catch me!'

'Hmm' mused Raymond, 'Not a pretty sight. Dented the old pride, eh? what?'

'Watch your tongue, you little pipsqueak, or I'll'…

'Or you'll what?' he sang, leaping suddenly from the bell-pull and landing neatly on the polished desk below. There he danced cheekily among sedate rows of marble eggs in tiny, gilded cups, sticking out his tongue and wagging his fingers at Dennis.

'Just you wait!' Dennis spat. Never had he been so cheeked by a mouse.

With great care, Raymond rolled one of the eggs to the edge and pushed it with all his might onto the unsuspecting Dennis, hitting him smack between the eyes. 'Take that!' he chortled, following it quickly with another egg which landed smartly on his nose. Then disaster! Raymond lost his footing and fell headlong onto the carpet. It felt like a long drop and his head swam as he tried to get up.

'Now who's boss?'

At once, Dennis pounced. With blood dripping from his nose, he scooped the little mouse up into his paws, 'Now who's boss?' he hissed.

Tossing Raymond into the air, he proceeded to kick him about like a football. 'Take that, and that, AND THAT!' he raged. Biff! Whack! Thump! Each kick winded poor Raymond terribly.

'Stop, stop, you brute' he cried before Dennis picked him up by his tail with a 'My, *my*, whatever's happened here? Let's see if we can straighten it, shall we?' as he twirled him round and round, faster and faster until a deep voice boomed 'What is all this caterwauling?'

Dennis spun round, dropping Raymond as Bunce the butler slid into view, his patent shoes squeaking importantly. 'Be off, Dennis, Her Majesty's had a long day. She mustn't be disturbed!' Dennis crawled away, loathe to admit defeat. He'd had a few run-ins with Bunce before and knew when to call it a day.

Bunce watched Dennis slope off down the corridor. Straightening his shoulders he knocked on the door. 'Your supper tray, Your Majesty' he said as he went in. Nervously, Raymond grabbed his case. As Bunce stepped forward, he stood in the open doorway, unable to move. His mouth felt dry and he shook all over. This was it! Here was the Queen at last. He could hardly believe his luck!

The patterned carpet beneath his feet felt thick and comforting. Around the room, soft lamps glowed on gilded cabinets. Heavy curtains shut out the sounds of London life. Only the ticking of a clock nearby broke the silence.

The Queen sat upright in a neat, gold chair. Her hair which was white and tightly curled framed her face like a snowy cap. Creamy pearls graced her neck while a sparkling diamond brooch was pinned to her dress. Sitting very still with her hands clasped in her lap, Raymond thought she looked quite wonderful.

Bunce bowed and placed the tray on a low table. 'Thank-you, Bunce. I'll ring for cocoa later' murmured the Queen. The door clicked shut. As she bent down to take off her shoes, she found herself looking straight at a small mouse in a tartan jacket, clutching a tiny case.

A countrywoman at heart, the Queen knew well the ways of mice and men. Calmly spreading her napkin on her lap she paused and said 'To whom do I owe this pleasure?'

'Raymond Mackenzie at your service, Your Majesty' came the reply.

Chapter Seven

Raymond meets the Queen!

The Queen smiled as Raymond stood to attention. She noticed that this small subject of hers had a tear in his jacket and that a lump was growing above his right eye.

'To my mind, Mr. Mackenzie, you look as if you've been in rather a fight!' she exclaimed.

Raymond's shoulders slumped. This was not a good beginning!

'I'm afraid, your Majesty, that I had a devil of a job getting past Dennis!'

'Ah, yes, Dennis is rather fiercesome! He seems to have spoiled your jacket!'

'My mother won't be best pleased. She had it specially made for me' he replied mournfully.

The Queen was touched. Even small mice had mothers and this one was no exception!

'Pray, Mr. Mackenzie, *do* sit down!'

'Oh, please, Ma'am, call me Raymond!'

'Very well' and here the Queen acted like the mother she was and offered Raymond a few tasty morsels from her plate by way of sustenance. That bucked him up no end!

And so, these two sat dining, the Queen in her comfy chair and Raymond on his little case. Just in time he remembered his mother's warning 'Never, *ever*, talk with your mouth full!'

At last the Queen spoke. 'Now Raymond, start from the beginning. Tell me about your family and why you're here.'

'Well, Ma'am, my grandmother, Maisie Mackenzie created the original recipes for *The Mackenzie Cheese Company* at her kitchen table.....'

'Do you mean that your family make cheeses?' enquired the Queen, trying not to smile.

'Yes, Ma'am, indeed we do. Papa Mackenzie, my grandfather, moved the business from Scotland and settled in London. We were very successful and had lots of customers. Sadly, sales have fallen recently. My father says that if something drastic doesn't happen soon, we'll be out on the streets!' he cried.

'I see,' replied the Queen. 'Would you be so kind as to show me what's in your case? I confess I'm quite curious!'

Up leapt Raymond and snapped open the locks with a flourish. Immediately he became quite the salesperson.

'For Your Majesty's delectation and delight, we have three of our finest cheeses on offer...'

'Oh,' said the Queen 'what have you called them?'

"*Balmoral Blue', 'Heather Breeze'* and *'Tam o' Shanter'!*"

'What wonderful names. They remind me of family holidays in Scotland. We had the greatest fun, they were the best of times' she said wistfully.

'Why, Your Majesty, I do think you need a bit of fun after your long day' and shaking off the dust of London streets, he bowed low and began to whistle a lively Scotch air.

Lifting his spindly arms above his head and pointing his toes, he began to leap higher and higher, twirling and skirling all the while, smacking his little tail emphatically on the ground to mark the beat!

Suddenly, the Queen couldn't help herself. Several explosive giggles escaped as a smile spread across her face and her eyes shone with joy. She began to sway from side to side and her feet tapped merrily.

As he skipped, Raymond fancied he saw the echo of a young Princess Elizabeth before him, who had danced like crazy on the streets of Piccadilly at the end of the war, when for one memorable evening, she tasted the freedom and joy of being among her people in a way she'd never known before.

Outside in the corridor, a new housemaid, dustpan in hand, sat back on her heels listening to the sounds of laughter and jollity from within. Her thin chest heaved and with a sigh, she shook her head in disbelief. 'Whatever next?' she said.

****

Raymond sat down on his case and wiped the sweat from his brow.

'However did you get past my guards?' asked the Queen. Raymond grinned. 'It was touch and go, Your Majesty. I found myself hanging from the end of a bayonet and thought it was all up for me! Then I mentioned my Uncle Archie and strangely that made the guard laugh! He ordered one of your footmen to take me down to the kitchens.'

'That uncle of yours is quite a character. I have a soft spot for him. We have some very lively conversations. He really makes me laugh' said the Queen. 'Now, Raymond' and here she looked at him kindly, 'How can I keep your family off the streets?'

Raymond stood up. His moment had come! He could almost feel the press of his father and grandfather at his back and the enormity of what he was about to ask made him tremble. When he spoke, however, he sounded calm.

'Would you do me the honour, Ma'am, of tasting our cheeses? If you like them, could you see your way to granting *The Mackenzie Cheese Company* a Royal Warrant?'

Slowly the Queen smiled. Opening each small packet, the creamy paper crackled beneath her fingers. With her butter knife she cut a piece from each cheese.

'Heather Breeze' she whispered. 'Mmm, this is creamy and I can almost smell the heather.

'Balmoral Blue' is rich, dense and full-bodied, it makes you sit up and take notice.

'Tam o' Shanter' is full of magic, it almost sets your pulses racing'…

Raymond's heart skipped a beat. 'She likes them!' he exclaimed to himself.

The Queen looked at her loyal subject standing before her. 'I have never tasted anything so delicious. These beautiful cheeses take me back to my childhood; they are simple, tasty and unforgettable!' Spurred into action the Queen dialled a number on her telephone, not unlike Uncle Archie's. Seconds ticked by.

'Ah, Purvis, would you be so good as to come up to the Blue Sitting-Room? I have an urgent matter for you to attend to' and with that, she replaced the receiver which settled into its cradle with a satisfying click! The ensuing silence held moments of rapture and suspense … presently there was a respectful knock at the door. 'Enter!' she replied.

****

When the call came to attend the Queen, her personal private secretary was just tucking into a tasty plate of fish and chips!

Friday night was fish night. All the staff looked forward to it, especially today, as they had been up since dawn, preparing a lavish luncheon for a well-known sheik and his entourage.

Purvis put down his knife and fork, wiped his mouth then checked in the mirror that there were no pieces of fish in his teeth! Why on earth had the Queen summoned him now? 'Whatever can it be?' he grumbled. 'She was fine when I left her this afternoon!'

As he entered the sitting-room, he looked around quickly and thought things looked pretty normal.

'Purvis, I would like you to meet a loyal subject of mine' and here the Queen indicated a small figure in a tartan jacket, sitting on a suitcase, very near Her Majesty's chair! 'This is Mr. Raymond Mackenzie of Kensal Rise...'

Purvis gulped and blinked at the Queen. What was all this? Why was she consorting with a common mouse and as for being a subject of hers! But he got no further.

'Mr. Mackenzie is related to Archibald Mackenzie, our trusty food taster, and as such is deserving of our help' and here the Queen fixed him with a steely look. Purvis knew better than to argue.

'What do you wish me to do, Your Majesty?' he asked.

'Please have a Royal Warrant drawn up *at once* for *The Mackenzie Cheese Company* of Kensal Rise, London. I have sampled their cheeses, they are simply delicious!'

Purvis felt as if his head was about to burst! The Queen was going to buy cheeses from a bunch of mice!

'But Ma'am' he stammered.

'Waste no time, Purvis,' commanded the Queen 'this request is to jump the queue!'

Purvis bowed.

'And Purvis,' she went on, 'it is getting late and Mr. Mackenzie needs to go home. We don't want his mother worrying on his behalf. Be so good as to have a car brought round in half an hour!' Then the Queen turned towards Raymond, 'Another Scotch air, if you please!' she said as Purvis backed out of the room.

Out in the corridor, he stood stock still, his heart thumped wildly and there was sweat on his brow. Quite simply, the Queen was asking him to bend the rules. No-one *ever* got a Royal Warrant straight away. What *was* he to do? In this unhappy state, he descended to his rooms and telephoned Bates the driver.

'Ah, Bates' he said. 'Be so good as to have a car ready in half an hour. The Queen has a special visitor who needs to go home…'

'But I thought all our guests had departed. Who on earth could it be, and at this hour too, when the Queen is having her supper?' he replied.

There was an awkward pause.

'It seems that Archie Mackenzie's nephew is with her.'

'What, a mouse?' he cried.

'Precisely, Bates!'

'Well I never. Our housemaid said at supper, she'd heard a lot of laughter coming from the sitting-room…'

'I have some urgent matters to attend to right now. I shall, however, accompany Mr. Mackenzie junior down to the car.'

'You can rely on me, Mr. Purvis' replied Bates.

He couldn't wait to tell everyone what was going on. Never in his time, as the Queen's chauffeur, had he been called upon to escort a mouse through the streets of London.

Things were looking up!

****

The Queen stood at the window looking down into the courtyard. She watched as Bates opened the car door and carefully helped Raymond in with his small case. It had been an extraordinary day!

'Where to, son?' asked Bates.

'Number 80, Kensal Crescent, if you please, sir!' he replied.

'Well, at least he has some manners,' thought Bates as he started the engine and disappeared into the dusky night.

Chapter Eight

Raymond gets his wish!

Mrs. Mackenzie stood at the kitchen sink. She stared out of the window. It was not yet dark. 'Oh, I do hope nothing has happened to him!' she sighed. She had been against sending Raymond to the palace but Mr. Mackenzie had been determined, 'He must go!'

A figure scurried past the window and banged on the front door. It was their

neighbour, Mrs. Jennings, a right, old busy-body. 'Mrs. Mackenzie, come quick! There's a posh car outside'…

A small crowd had gathered on the pavement as Mrs. Mackenzie pushed her way through.

'It's got the Royal Coat of Arms on the door!' someone cried.

'But there's no-one inside!' shouted another.

Mrs. Mackenzie gasped. This was no ordinary car. 'What was the proper term?' she asked herself. 'Ah, yes, it's a limousine, that's it!'

'What's going on?' snapped Mr. Mackenzie.

'Sshh' went his wife. 'Wait and see!'

'Oooh', went the spectators. 'Look, look!'

Now a small face could been seen at the window. Raymond raised a hand and waved majestically. With great ceremony Bates the driver walked smartly around to the front of the car, 'Silence, please!' he commanded as he opened the door, unfolding a small set of steps. There, at the top, stood Raymond, case in hand. In a clear voice, he looked up at Bates. 'Thank-you, sir, for seeing me home safely. Please also thank Her Majesty for making it possible'… and here he stepped down straight into the arms of his waiting mother.

****

After the royal car departed and their neighbours drifted away, the family crowded around Raymond desperate to hear how he had got on at the palace.

Shaking with excitement, he drew a white card from his pocket and read out the following:-

'What?' gasped Mr. Mackenzie, 'does this mean…?'

'Yes, father' Raymond replied, 'the Queen loved our cheeses so much she wants to present us with the Royal Warrant herself!'

There were shouts of joy as Clarissa danced round the room, baby George clapped his hands and Papa Mac cried gleefully 'We've *done* it, we've *done* it!'

****

And so it was!

Dressed in their best, the Mackenzie family showed up at the palace. With Uncle Archie on hand to guide them through the maze of rooms and corridors, they found themselves at last in the presence of Her Majesty the Queen.

As she handed Mr. Mackenzie the Royal Warrant, the Queen smiled kindly at him:-

'It gives me *great* pleasure to present *The Mackenzie Cheese Company* with this special award.

Young Raymond cheered me up after an extremely tiring day. You should be very proud of him!

Congratulations to you all and Good Luck for the future!'

****

Lord Chamberlain's Office

This is to certify by command of
The Queen
I have appointed
The Mackenzie Cheese Company
into the place and quality of
Cheese Manufacturers
to Her Majesty

This Warrant is granted to
Hector Mackenzie Esquire

———————————

Given under my hand and seal this — day of —— 2016 in the sixty-third year of Her Majesty's Reign.

Lord Chamberlain

After the ceremony, they tucked into a splendid tea with scones, jam and cream aplenty while Uncle Archie entertained them with tales of his adventures in the Far East.

And it was generally agreed by the Queen's servants that it was the funniest, jolliest party that they had ever seen at the palace for many a long year!